Ho diddle-ho and
A hey diddle-hey,
Weigh the anchor,
We sail today.

Hey diddle-hey,
A ho diddle-ho,
Set the sails...
And off we go!

American edition published in 2016 by Andersen Press USA, an imprint of Andersen Press Ltd.
www.andersenpressusa.com

First published in Great Britain in 2015 by Andersen Press Ltd., 20 Vauxhall Bridge Road, London SW1V 2SA.

Distributed in the United States and Canada by Lerner Publishing Group, Inc. 241 First Avenue North
Minneapolis, MN 55401 USA
For reading levels and more information, look up this title at www.lernerbooks.com.

Color separated in Switzerland by Photolitho AG, Zürich. Printed and bound in Malaysia by Tien Wah Press.

Library of Congress Cataloging-in-Publication Data Available.
ISBN: 978-1-5124-0427-2, eBook ISBN: 978-1-5124-0446-3
1-TWP-7/1/15

Ahoy there, first mate Herbie - G.P.J.

Avast ye, young sea dogs Codie and Kyle - G.P.

Are You The PIRATE CAPTAIN?

Gareth P. Jones   Garry Parsons

ANDERSEN PRESS

"This pirate ship be ready,"
hollered First Mate Hugh.
"We've hammered nails, chipped off the snails,
and even washed the crew."

"We've **mopped** and **swabbed** and scrubbed it.
We've cleaned the crow's nest out.
There's one thing though, before we go,
that we **can't** do without."

Last Sighting of
Captain
Sid

by First Mate Hugh

"We all recall our last one –
that Scurvy Sea Dog Sid.

Never beaten till he got eaten by that giant squid."

The pirates sat there waiting
till First Mate Hugh cried,

"Look!"

"You see that guy
who's rowing by?
His left hand is a hook!"

"Are you the Pirate Captain?
Your hook is quite a sight. Was it a shark
that left its mark in some almighty fight?"

The man said, "I'm no pirate. This here's a pleasure boat."

"And what you took to be a hook is a hanger for my coat."

The next chap had a parrot.
Hugh yelled, "It must be fate!"

"In fact I'll bet
this pirate's pet
will squawk,
'Pieces of eight.'"

"Are you the Pirate Captain?"

"Not at all, young fella.
How absurd!
It's clear this bird
is part of my umbrella."

Along the docks a man held
a scroll torn down the fold.

Scurvy Sid's

Gold be in the

"Our missing scrap of treasure map!
It's sure to lead to gold."

"Are you the Pirate Captain –
our map clutched in your fist?"

"This ain't no map," replied the chap. "This here's me shopping list."

Then in the gloom they spotted
a glistening silver blade,
two gold teeth and underneath,
a beard tied in a braid!

"Are you the Pirate Captain?"

"Sadly no, m'hearty.
This pirate gear I'm wearing here
is for a dress-up party."

"Who got this ship all shipshape? Who organized the crew?
Who mopped the sails, removed the snails?"

"Who? I ask you, who?"

The **pirates** had the **answer.**
"We **know** what we must do.
We've **all** agreed
the one to **lead**..."

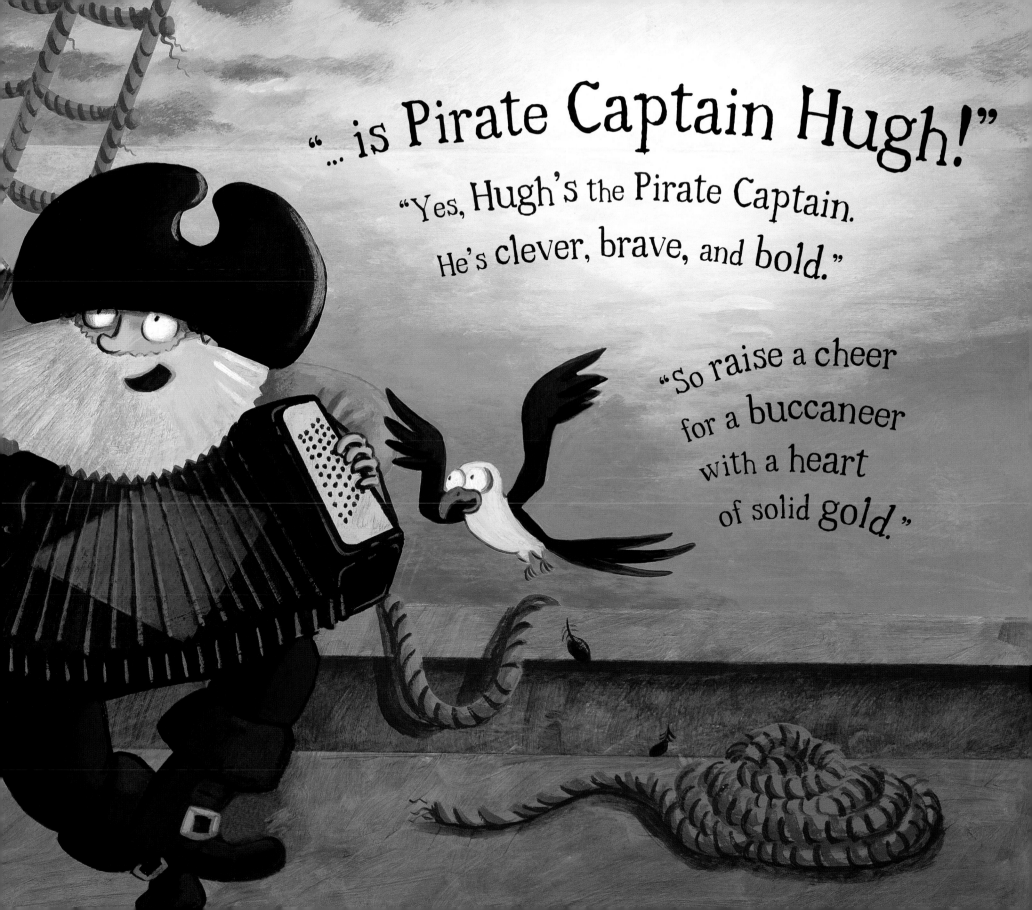

"... is Pirate Captain Hugh!"

"Yes, Hugh's the Pirate Captain. He's clever, brave, and bold."

"So raise a cheer for a buccaneer with a heart of solid gold."